TH
BEARS'
BLITZ

THE BEARS' BLITZ

AND OTHER SPORTS STORIES
Compiled by the Editors
of
Highlights for Children

BOYDS MILLS PRESS

Compilation copyright © 1992 by Boyds Mills Press, Inc.
Contents copyright by Highlights for Children, Inc.
All rights reserved
Published by Boyds Mills Press, Inc.
A Highlights Company
815 Church Street
Honesdale, Pennsylvania 18431
Printed in the United States of America
Publisher Cataloging-in-Publication Data.
Main entry under title.

   Bears' blitz : and other sports stories / compiled by the Editors
of Highlights for Children.
[96] p. : ill. ;   cm.
Stories originally published in Highlights for Children.
Summary: A collection of stories on various sports, including baseball,
soccer, hockey, swimming, and skiing.
ISBN 1-878093-29-0
[1. Sports stories] I. Highlights for Children. II. Title.
                [F]   1992
Library of Congress Catalog Card Number: 90-85908

Drawings by Judith Hunt
Distributed by St. Martin's Press

      4 5 6 7 8 9 10

Highlights® is a registered trademark of Highlights for Children, Inc.

CONTENTS

The Bears' Blitz by Stephanie Moody 7

Way to Go, Tracy! by Isobel Morin 13

Roberto and the Soccer Game
by Bernadine Beatie 19

High-Tower Lie by Jeanne Blumenthal....................27

The New Skater by Dorothy Boys Kilian 35

Beverley's Tall Story by Ann Bixby Herold.............41

On His Toes by Linda McCollum Brown...................47

The Smallest Surfer by Rick Boyes........................53

Dogsled Race by Iris Klapka 59

The Relay Race by Isobel Morin.............................65

Sweet September by Robert Anderson 71

Ski Tracks on Silver Bell by Jean Heyn 77

The Girl Who Couldn't Stop Reading
by Nancy West 85

Sea Legs by Carolyn Bowman....................................91

The Bears' Blitz

By Stephanie Moody

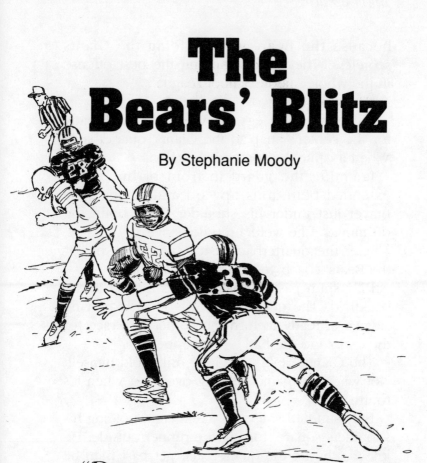

"DE-fense. DE-fense." The steady chanting of the Bears' football fans cut through the cool autumn night.

Moving into his defensive position, Billy glanced up at the scoreboard. He knew what it said—zero to zero—but he still liked to look, because the Bears were holding the Giants scoreless. They were stopping the best offense in the whole Middle School League.

"Hut one. Hut two."

Billy tensed his legs. He was coiled and ready for the center's snap to the Giants' quarterback. When it came, he sprang into action.

Jamming the guard in front of him, Billy extended both arms upward and popped the player just under his shoulder pads, bouncing off him as if he were a red-hot stove.

"Get the quarterback. Sack the quarterback!" the Bears' coach yelled from the sidelines.

Billy spun past his blocker and looked in the backfield. The quarterback was already moving sideways, ready to turn the corner and race for the end zone. He had to be stopped.

The Giants can't score now, Billy told himself. Not when the game's almost over. Not when it's fourth down.

Billy shuffled sideways like a crab, holding his shoulders square, forcing the runner outside. He knew if he let the quarterback get past him, he would need a motorcycle to catch up. Billy wasn't fast, but he was big. He was strong.

Keeping his eyes glued to the quarterback, he settled into his hitting position, watching the player's belt buckle, ready for the fake.

BAM! Billy hit the runner hard with his

shoulder, using his legs to drive the quarterback upward and back. Two of his teammates joined in the tackle.

"What a hit!" yelled Jack, helping Billy up from the pile of players. "Give me five, man. Give me five," Jack chanted. "We held 'em."

Billy traded high fives with his best friend as they trotted off the field. Now it was the offense's turn. If only they would score. If only the Bears could win.

Billy couldn't believe his team hadn't won a game all season. They hadn't even scored! It was embarrassing.

"I wish I could get my hands on that ball," Billy said to Jack as they crouched on the sidelines, watching the game. "I wish *I* could play quarterback."

"Yeah, and I'd be your running back," Jack said.

"Why not?" asked Billy, "Think of it. I'd take the snap, tucking the ball in, spinning loose, running, leaping over the line . . . and if I got in trouble, you'd be there to help me."

"Dream on, man," Jack said. "I'm the free safety. You're a linebacker. We play *defense,* not offense."

"But . . ."

"No buts. That's the way Coach wants it. That's the way it is."

"Fumble!" cried Billy, jumping to his feet.

"Oh, no," moaned Jack. "We're in again."

"Hey, you. Jack! Billy!" The coach's gruff voice punched through the crowd's roar. "We gotta blitz, boys. Shake 'em up." The coach pointed at the game clock. "Time's running out. Get the ball back. You can do it."

Billy and Jack raced onto the field. "Pressure the quarterback," Billy said in the huddle. "Get a fence around him. Get that ball."

Watching for the snap, Billy smacked into the line when the center hiked the ball. Pushing, twisting, Billy plowed forward, trying to get through. The center and a guard shut him out. The Bears' blitz wasn't working. The Giants were trying a screen play, a short pass. Spinning to the side, Billy ricocheted off the blockers and leaped into the air. His hands slapped into the loose ball, shooting it straight up. He saw his chance. Cupping his hands together, Billy netted the tumbling ball with his fingers.

"Run!" the fans cheered. "Run!"

Billy's heart boomed in his chest. He had the ball. He could score.

Sprinting down the field, Billy tucked the ball into his body. Giants were behind him: two on his left, one on his right. He could hear their feet pounding on the turf. He had to outrun them, but the goal line was so far away.

Glancing to his left, Billy saw a Giants jersey closing in on him, and hands reaching out to grab him.

He veered to the right, lengthening his stride, panting for breath.

"Hey, need some help?"

Billy gasped. It was Jack, just behind him on his right! Jack could block the Giants. Jack could . . .

Billy loosened his grip on the football. He knew what to do. Tossing the ball laterally into his friend's waiting hands, Billy crashed into the blue jersey on his left, knocking the player off stride and giving Jack some running room.

Jack galloped the final yards to the end zone, holding the ball up in a victory salute.

Billy and the Bears went wild, jumping up and down, whooping for joy. They had scored! Billy scampered into the end zone, whirled his best friend around, and pounded him on the back. "Give me five, Jack. Give me five," he said, repeating Jack's favorite phrase.

"I just gave you *six*!" Jack shouted, hugging Billy. "I guess wishes really can come true."

Billy laughed out loud, staring up at the scoreboard, watching it change the Bears' zero to a six. "Yeah," he said finally, grinning from ear to ear. "With a little help from my friends, wishes *can* come true."

Way to Go, Tracy!

By Isobel Morin

Tracy Blair's bat smacked the softball, sending it soaring into the air. The Cardinals' center fielder watched helplessly as the ball sailed over the fence for a home run.

As Tracy crossed home plate to score the winning run for the Glenview Tigers, her teammates mobbed her, yelling and pounding her on the back. Thanks to Tracy's home run, the Tigers would play Smithtown for the county championship.

When the hubbub died down, Mrs. Keen, the Tigers' coach, hugged Tracy and said, "Way to go! If you play as well in the championship as you did today, the Tigers are sure to win."

On the way home, Tracy thought of the beautiful trophy each member of the winning team would receive. She could picture one sitting in the trophy case beside her big brother Kevin's baseball trophies. She was always glad for Kevin when he won another award, but she longed to have a trophy of her own.

Tracy was crossing her lawn when her five-year-old neighbor ran to her, crying loudly.

"What's the matter, Krista?" asked Tracy.

"My kitten is stuck in our tree, and Grandma can't get him down," wailed Krista, pulling on Tracy's arm.

Tracy followed Krista into her backyard. Sure enough, Krista's grandmother was trying to reach the tiny striped kitten, which clung to a branch, mewing in fright. "Don't worry," Tracy told them. "I'll get him down."

Tracy dragged a picnic bench over to the tree and climbed onto it. She reached up to grab the kitten, but it scrambled farther up the tree, beyond her reach.

"I'll climb up," Tracy said. She shinnied up the tree trunk until she was able to grasp the lowest branch. Then she climbed until she reached the branch where the kitten was crouching. Tracy edged her way over to it, calling softly as she went. When she got within grabbing distance, she snatched the struggling ball of fur with one hand and held onto the branch with the other.

The frightened kitten suddenly dug its claws into Tracy's arm. She yelled and let go of the branch. Down Tracy tumbled, still clutching the kitten. As she crash-landed on the dry grass, she felt a sharp twinge in her ankle. Tracy tried to stand, but she flopped down, yelping in pain.

Later that afternoon Tracy sat on the sun porch, scowling at the swollen ankle propped on a hassock. Only a sprain, Dr. Chang had said. Only! It would never heal in time for her to play in the championship. The game was on Sunday, only three days away. She would miss her chance to help the Tigers win. If only she hadn't climbed the tree. The kitten probably would have come down by itself anyway.

Kevin came home from his summer job at the Pizza Palace. He rumpled Tracy's hair and said, "Tough luck, champ, but you'll get a chance to play in the championship next year."

"Maybe," replied Tracy with a weak smile. It didn't help ease her disappointment.

After supper Tracy's teammates Beth and Sarah came over to visit. As they drank glasses of Kevin's super-duper special lemonade, Beth asked, "Will you come to the game on Sunday anyway, even though you can't play?"

Tracy looked at the crutches propped beside her chair. "I don't know," she said. "It's hard to get around on these things."

"Oh, please come and cheer for the Tigers," said Sarah.

Tracy sighed. "All right," she answered.

On Sunday afternoon Tracy sat on the front steps while Dad backed the car out of the garage. She glared at the bright sunshine. She hated the thought of sitting on the bench while the rest of the Tigers swung bats, ran bases, and chased balls.

Krista ran over, her kitten clutched tightly against her chest. "Thank you for saving my kitty," she said.

Tracy gently loosened Krista's grip on the kitten. "That's okay," she replied. "But don't hold him so tightly. Remember that he's only a baby."

Tracy wondered whether she should find some excuse for staying home. Maybe she could say her ankle hurt too much. No, she decided, that wouldn't be fair. She would go and cheer for her team. Tracy grabbed her crutches and hobbled to the car.

Dad pulled the car over close to the Glenview High School softball field. Kevin hopped out and opened the door for Tracy, then helped her over to the Tigers' bench.

A lawn chair sat at one end of the bench. It was decorated with blue and yellow crepe paper—the Tigers' team colors. Blue and yellow balloons were tied to its back. Coach Keen helped Tracy into the chair, and her teammates crowded around her.

Sarah handed Tracy a box wrapped in blue paper and tied with a yellow ribbon. Tracy opened it, and there, nestled in folds of tissue paper, lay a small trophy engraved with the words "Tracy Blair, Glenview Tigers' Most Valuable Player."

The Tigers cheered. Tracy grinned. "All right, Tigers!" she shouted. "Let's win this game!"

Roberto and the Soccer Game

By Bernadine Beatie

Roberto stood close to the front of a long line of people waiting to buy tickets. Though he had ridden all night on the small bus that traveled from his village to the city, he was much too excited to be tired. Today Roberto's dream would come true. At long last he would see a soccer game between the two finest teams in Brazil! It hadn't been easy. First he'd had to persuade his parents that he was old enough to come alone; then he'd had to earn the money. Roberto grinned and moved a step forward.

"Is it always so hard to get tickets?" Roberto asked the tall man next in line.

"Not always. We are lucky to be so near the head of the line. Many behind us will be turned away." The man shrugged. "When Jorge Santos plays, everyone wants to see him."

Roberto smiled. He had cut many pictures of Jorge Santos from newspapers. "Someday," Roberto said, "I am going to be a soccer player."

The man's reply was lost in a burst of cheering. The street was suddenly filled with young men and boys, shouting and laughing, running beside a long black car.

"Santos! Jorge Santos!" A great shout went up.

Roberto's heart pounded. Jorge Santos sat, tall and proud, on the back seat of the car. He was waving and smiling.

Roberto would have dashed forward to join the crowd, but the tall man caught his arm. "Don't lose your place. Soon the tickets will be gone."

As Roberto stepped back into line, he saw that a shabbily dressed old man, leaning heavily on a cane, was being swept along by the crowd.

"Careful!" Roberto called. But no one heard, and Roberto saw the old man stumble and fall. Then the crowd surged forward, hiding him from view. Roberto forgot everything. He left his place in line, squirmed through the crowd, and knelt beside the old man.

"Are you hurt, *senhor*?" he asked.

The old man was red-faced and angry. "Help me up! Fetch my cane!" he cried crossly.

When Roberto obeyed, instead of thanking him, the old man glared at him. He raised his cane and shook it at the crowd that followed Jorge Santos.

"Villains! Scoundrels!" he yelled. "Why don't you look where you're going?" He leaned heavily on Roberto's arm. "There's a bench at the corner of the stadium," he said. "Help me to it."

"But, *senhor*—" Roberto looked over his shoulder. The line waiting for tickets was even longer now.

"You knocked me down," the old man said impatiently. "The least you can do is take me someplace where I can rest a moment and get my breath."

Roberto looked back again. He gave a little cry of dismay as the ticket window slammed shut and a Sold Out sign flashed on. There were a few scattered boos, and the crowd started moving away.

"What are you waiting for? Come along," the old man ordered.

Roberto's heart was in his stomach. He had given up his chance to see the game just to help this cross old man. For a moment he thought of running away, of letting the old man get to the bench the best way he could. Roberto shrugged. That would serve no purpose now that the tickets were gone. And there was such a crowd about them that he was afraid the man might fall again. So he walked slowly, keeping his shoulder high to support the man.

The old man kept up a steady grumbling. "Young people! All they think about is games and excitement. Think of the money they will waste today on foolishness!"

Roberto noticed again how shabbily he was dressed. He was probably cross because he had no money. He might even be hungry.

"Here," Roberto said, thrusting part of his money into the old man's hand. "I don't need it now."

There was a startled look on the man's face. "I do not need your money," he said gruffly.

The crowd was so thick now that they had to pause. And over the heads of those nearest to him, Roberto suddenly saw the tall man who had stood next to him in line.

"I told you," the man cried, "if you lost your

place in line you would not get a ticket!" Then the man was pushed along by the crowd.

"Ha!" said the old man. "So that is why you no longer need your money." He laughed softly. "You gave up your place in line to help me, and you have stayed with me even though I have been cross and unreasonable. Why?"

Roberto searched for words.

"Never mind," the old man said. "It is enough that you did it." He chuckled softly. "Come, follow me. You shall see the game."

"But the tickets are all gone, *senhor*!" Roberto cried.

"Nonsense!" exclaimed the old man, pushing Roberto toward the entrance of the stadium. "Who needs tickets?"

The old man must have lost his mind! Roberto tried to pull away, but the man propelled him forward. And when they walked through the entrance to the stadium, Roberto could hardly believe his eyes. The uniformed attendants bowed and smiled, clearing a way for them. The next thing Roberto knew, the old man was steering him through a corridor that led to the rooms where the players were waiting for the game to start.

"*Senhor* Gomez!" rang out from all sides.

Roberto swallowed. "Ernesto Gomez?" he asked in a small voice.

"None other!" One of the players came over and gave the old man a hug. "And still going around dressed like a pauper."

Roberto gasped. The speaker was Jorge Santos! And Ernesto Gomez, this poor old man, was the owner of Jorge's team!

Senhor Gomez laughed. "This way I can find out what people really think of my team." He looked down at Roberto. "But today, had it not been for this one, I would have been trampled on the street. He gave up his chance to get a ticket so that he could help me."

"You shall have the best seat in the house."

Jorge grinned down at Roberto. "You shall sit on the bench beside us."

Roberto's heart was so full he couldn't speak. He smiled shyly at Jorge and at *Senhor* Gomez. It was not every day that dreams came true!

High-Tower Lie

By Jeanne Blumenthal

Jenny biked to Thomas Beach every day with her two best friends. But Jenny was far too restless to just lie in the sun with Elly and Barb. She was a good swimmer, so she was allowed to swim past the ropes and out to the float. Jenny liked to perch on a corner and watch for divers trying the high tower. Most people went off the board on the edge of the float, under the high tower. In Jenny's eyes, the handful of people she had seen go off the high tower were very brave.

One afternoon Jenny sat drying on the edge of the float, hoping someone would go off the tower. It was nearly time to go home. The float was deserted except for Jenny and B.T., the lifeguard. Jenny stood up, eyeing the high tower.

"Won't hurt to go up the ladder," B.T. said.

Jenny said nothing, but her eyes followed each rung of the ladder up to the top. It was high, all right. She looked back at B.T. He was watching her with a smile that seemed to say, Look, kid, we both know you're pretending. But I'll go along with you.

I'll show him, Jenny thought. She approached the ladder and started to climb, not looking back at B.T. On top, Jenny's first impulse was to grab something to hang on to. There was nothing but sunny space. The beach looked far away. Then she looked down. That was a mistake. A light, giddy feeling filled her, and she quickly crouched down and carefully backed up to the ladder and scampered down.

B.T. was laughing, but when he saw her face he stopped. "Hey, kid. You all right?"

Jenny nodded.

"It takes some getting used to," he said. "Don't let it get you."

That evening at dinner Jenny was unusually quiet. David, her brother, announced that he had been given a raise in pay, and Sylvia, her sister, happily announced that she had finally found a job.

"We're a family of doers," Mr. Anderson said, proud and pleased. "And what about you, Jen? At the beach again?"

"I went off the high tower today," Jenny blurted out—and was immediately sorry.

"No kidding, Jen. Are you sure you're not adding a few feet to your dock dive? I never went off the high one and I know Sylvia hasn't," David said.

"Me, go off the high tower?" Sylvia said, rolling her eyes to the ceiling. "I have trouble just making it out to the ropes."

"Now that's really something, Jen," Mr. Anderson said. "What do you say we all go to the beach after dinner and watch Jenny do her stuff?"

"Oh, you don't have to do that," Jenny said weakly. "It's not such a big deal."

"Well, I can't go. I have a date," said Sylvia. "Sorry, Jen."

"Me too, Jen," David said apologetically. "Tennis in an hour, but I'll go next time to be sure you're not just bragging again."

"And I have a library board meeting," Mrs.

Anderson added. Jenny perked up noticeably. Saved, she thought.

"So," continued Mr. Anderson, "that leaves just you and me."

"Hey, Dad," David said, "I never knew the high tower meant so much to you."

"It's not the high tower itself," he answered as he watched Jenny. "It's the overcoming of an obstacle."

A storm, Jenny thought an hour later on the drive to the beach. I wish for a big electrical storm. Or even just some rain. Dad would never let us be out in the water during the rain.

"I guess we're ahead of the evening crowd," Mr. Anderson said as he pulled into a parking spot. "Let's go! I'll swim out with you," he said happily.

In no hurry to reach the float, Jenny swam smoothly and easily. The only thing that will save me now, she thought, is a cramp . . . an awful, painful cramp. She thought of faking it, but she knew her father wouldn't believe it. She wouldn't lie again. On the float, she thought, I'll just tell him the truth. I don't know what he'll do, but I just can't go off that high tower. She looked up at the tower and quickly stuck her face back in the water.

"That felt good, but I'm winded," her father said as they stood on the float. "Ready?"

"Dad? I . . ." He looked at her and waited silently. B.T. sat in his chair watching them. A few swimmers were resting on the edge of the float.

I just can't, Jenny thought. I just can't tell him in front of all these people. She smiled weakly, and her father patted her shoulder.

"It's okay," Mr. Anderson said.

When she was halfway up the ladder, B.T. called out to her.

It took me longer to get up here this afternoon, Jenny thought as she straightened up and took a few deep breaths. She knew everyone on the dock was looking up at her, and she didn't want to see them. Instead, she looked down at the water. It seemed a hundred miles away! "Oh, don't let me get dizzy," she whispered. "Please don't let me get dizzy."

Her legs felt weak and shaky as she stepped forward to the edge of the board. She tried hard to remember everything she had been taught about diving. After all, she thought, I've had plenty of practice, and I know what to do.

Raising her arms, she was aware that they were trembling. She pressed the palms of her hands together in front of her to steady her arms, took a deep breath, swallowed her fear, raised her arms, and sprang off the board.

Down, down, down. It seemed forever. She thought her hands would never cut the water. Then, suddenly, the impact of the water, slick and smooth. As the force of the descent weakened, Jenny opened her arms, pushing against the water to stop herself from going farther down, and started to push up. She felt as if her lungs were going to burst if she held her breath a second longer. Fear returned. I'm not going to make it. I'm not going to make it. Without warning, she broke the surface of the water and gasped for breath.

The onlookers shouted hurrahs as Jenny flipped over on her back and gently floated to catch her breath. I'll never take that tower again, she vowed.

On the drive home Jenny was silent. As they pulled into the driveway, Mr. Anderson said, "You know, Jen, I really thought that this time you had boasted yourself into a corner." Startled, Jenny could only stare at her father.

As he turned off the ignition, he said, "I thought that once you got to the tower you'd turn back. I thought I was going to teach you a good lesson."

"Daddy," she answered, "sometimes people have to learn their own lessons."

Mr. Anderson broke out in a wide grin. "Jen, we're a lot alike, you and I."

The New Skater

By Dorothy Boys Kilian

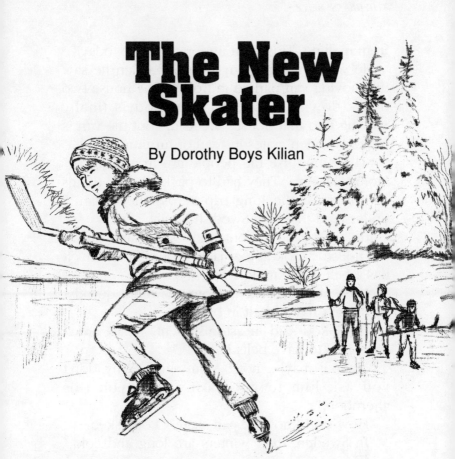

Rod tossed his ice skates over his shoulder as he hurried out of the house.

"Better pull your collar up," Mom warned him from the front door. "There's a cold wind blowing."

"I'm glad there is," Rod said. "It'll keep the ice

from melting. This is an important game today."

He was starting down the steps when he saw the moving van parked in front of the house two doors down the street. "Somebody's finally moving into that house," he said. "But the van is full of wooden crates instead of furniture."

"That's because the people are from Europe," Mom told him. "They had to pack all their things in boxes for the long trip across the ocean. I understand they're a Swedish family."

Just then a boy about Rod's size came out of the house. "Look at that jacket!" Rod laughed. "It has a belt in the middle of the back."

"Look at your jacket," Mom answered quickly. "It doesn't have a belt in back."

"But," Rod said in astonishment, "coats aren't supposed to have belts in back."

"Maybe, maybe not," Mom said. "Why don't you ask him to go skating with you this afternoon?"

"How do I know he can skate?" Rod asked.

"In Sweden, their winters are long and cold," said Mom.

"He probably can't speak English," Rod muttered.

"People can understand a lot from each other without words, if they really want to," said Mom.

"The thing is, Mom," Rod protested, "we're having this big hockey game today with the kids from over on Lambert Street, and he'd just get in our way."

Mom was quiet for a minute. Then she went in the house and closed the door.

Rod shrugged his shoulders and started down the front walk. He'd have to hurry now to get to the pond in time for the game.

As he came to the moving van, he saw the new boy staring at his skates. "Hi," Rod said uncomfortably. He felt he had to say something, since he was going right past.

The boy's blue eyes lighted up. "Hi," he answered.

Rod kept walking, but not quite as fast. He could almost feel the boy's eyes boring into his back where his skates were clanking together against his jacket. Slowly he stopped and turned around. He took a few steps back. The boy was smiling now, a little shyly.

Rod took a deep breath. "I'm Rod," he said, pointing a mittened hand toward himself.

The boy smiled. "Gunnar," he said, pointing to himself and ducking his blond head in an awkward bow.

"You have skates?" Rod asked, holding his own pair up between them.

"*Ja.*" Gunnar nodded excitedly, waving an arm toward one of the wooden boxes that had just been unloaded from the van. He picked up a crowbar that was lying on the ground and stuck it into the crate. Rod stepped over and helped push down on the bar until, with a wrenching screech, the top of the crate flew open. Gunnar reached in and pulled out a bulging flannel bag. Triumphantly he took out of it a pair of gleaming black-and-silver skates.

He looked so happy that Rod took him by the arm. "Come with me?" he asked. Just as Mom had said, people seemed to understand without knowing a lot of each other's language.

Gunnar ran into his house and came out a minute later with a lady who looked at Rod, smiled, and said "*Ja,* you go," as she gave Gunnar a little push forward.

Well, Rod thought, as the boys started off together, the gang would probably be mad because he was so late getting to the pond, and they wouldn't be too happy about his bringing along a stranger. But he'd just have to make the best of it.

"Where've you been?" Rod's friends called impatiently as Rod and Gunnar came through the park to the pond. "We're all ready to play."

Rod knelt down quickly to put on his skates. "This is Gunnar. He's from Sweden. He doesn't speak much English," he explained. The boys nodded at Gunnar and stared.

"Well, hurry up and get those skates on," Tom

Phillips said. "We're one man short as it is. Mike couldn't come this afternoon."

One man short! Rod stood up on his skates and looked at Gunnar. "You play?" he asked, handing him a stick. Gunnar grinned, grabbed hold of the stick, and glided out on the ice.

"Aw, he doesn't know how to play," Tom protested. "He'll just get in our way."

"Wow," yelled one of the other boys, "look at him go!"

Rod and the others stared out over the pond. Gunnar was already down at the other end, pushing a can in front of him. With ice shavings flying out from under his skates, he made a whooshing right-about turn and raced back toward them. As he came, he gave the can a mighty whack that sent it spinning right under their noses.

"It's a good thing you brought your new friend, Rod," Tom said sheepishly after a second of amazed silence. "With him playing, the game's as good as won."

"I guess skating is skating, American or Swedish style," Rod said happily as he picked up his own stick and joined Gunnar on the ice.

Beverley's Tall Story

By Ann Bixby Herold

Did you ever see one of those movies where they show a plant growing?

You know what I mean.

A shoot pops out of the ground, the leaves take ten seconds to unwrap themselves, and the next thing you know, it's a sunflower eight feet tall.

My brother John says that if you could get kids to stand still long enough, you could film them growing, too. He says I would be a good subject. He got the idea when Grandpa said I was growing like a weed. John swears he

41

watched me grow a whole inch one morning, waiting for the school bus. He even offered me a share in the fortune he is going to make from the movie.

John is nine, and he thinks he's a genius.

He can be convincing, but mostly his plans fall apart. Like the movie. Everything was fine until he found out the camera would cost two thousand dollars.

It's true I've been growing faster than anyone else I know. For years I was the same size as my two best friends. Then, suddenly, I was the tallest girl in my class. Almost overnight I grew taller than Mike Boswell, the tallest boy. It was frightening! Mike thinks he's something special. *I* think he's boring.

I'll never forget the look he gave me the day I stood next to him in the cafeteria.

"Have I shrunk?" he asked.

His friends fell all over the place laughing. I stepped on his foot. Hard. Accidentally, of course.

"How's the weather up there, Beverley?" he yelled. He has a *very* original mind.

"Watch out, there's a storm coming," I said, cool as you please. This time *my* friends laughed.

It was depressing. When I wasn't walking around with my knees bent, I was wearing out my brain cells thinking of comebacks to all the stupid comments. None of my clothes fit me for more than five minutes. And I broke so many things Dad called me a one-person demolition derby.

My whole life was falling apart. While Dad made jokes, Mom told me I was lucky!

"I always wanted to be tall," she said.

That's easy for someone only five foot two to say. I know what it's like when you're eleven and your mother's clothes are too small for you. It's embarrassing.

The worst thing was that I'd already planned my future. I wanted to be a famous ballet dancer. I'd been taking lessons for years, and I'd won some prizes. But, as John said, whoever heard of a giant ballerina? I even had a nightmare about it. At my debut in New York I did a grand jeté, and my head crashed into the overhead scenery. Then Mikhail Baryshnikov came on stage to be my partner, and he was carrying a ladder.

Waking up didn't help. My bed had shrunk.

And when my ballet teacher started shaking her head and telling the others to move back and give me more room, I knew my ballet days were numbered.

John and I were out in the backyard. I was walking around with a big rock on my head. I'd read someplace that heavy weights can slow a person's growth.

John was doing two of his favorite things: working his way through a bag of peanuts and pestering me. He sprawled on the grass at my feet, munching like a hamster.

"You *are* tall," he said for the millionth time. "From down here you look like a giant redwood."

I returned the rock to the rock garden. Then I walked over, stuck out my arms, yelled "TIMBER!" and fell on him.

"Have you gone bananas?" he gasped when I rolled off and helped myself to the last peanuts.

"They chopped me down," I said happily.

It's not often I catch John off guard.

My brother *hates* to change the subject.

"I bet you end up seven feet tall, Bev. Maybe ten! At night through my bedroom wall I can hear your bones growing."

"You can not!"

"I can too. They make the weirdest noises. Like someone being stretched on the rack. Creek. Groan. Creeeee . . . ."

Even a genius has trouble talking with someone sitting on his head.

"I'm going to forgive you," he said grandly when I'd let him up, "because I'm going to be your manager and make you famous."

Instantly I was on guard. With John you have to be.

"What for? Being tall?"

"Kind of. If you grow *real* tall, you could be a world-class basketball player."

"Basketball? I'm no good at team sports."

"How do you know? You've never tried. All you ever did was *ballet*." He looked disgusted.

"I'm not coordinated."

"You were once. You can be again *if* you ever stop growing."

"Of course I'll stop! Dr. Hallam says I'll be about six feet."

"How does she know that? The taller, the better. Fetch the basketball, and let's see what you can do. There's no time to lose."

It's always best to go along with John when he gets his wild ideas. So I tried basketball and, you know, it can be fun. I've been playing ever since.

John resigned as my manager last week. He said I wasn't growing fast enough. He got all upset when I refused to do any stretching exercises.

I'm still the tallest girl in class, but two boys have overtaken me. Mike has stopped his stupid jokes. Not that I care. I've just made the basketball team.

I'm thinking of working towards the Olympics.

On His Toes

By Linda McCollum Brown

This whole mess started just because I'm left-handed.

Last month Tim and Jeff talked me into signing up for Little League. Now baseball is okay and all, but it isn't my favorite thing to do. Just give me my clarinet or a chemistry set or a tennis racket or a book to read—especially a mystery—and Mike Marino is happy. But Tim and Jeff are my best friends, and they said that a lefty can really do a right-handed pitcher in and that I could help their team out a whole lot.

47

So, I figured, why not? The Panthers' coach, Mr. Goodwin, said, "Hey, great—Mike's a southpaw!" I can't stand it when people call me a southpaw (I mean, does that make them northpaws?), but other than that, Mr. Goodwin is okay. He is a real strong ballplayer, a super athlete.

Mom said I could ride the bus to practice so I wouldn't have to bother Mrs. Neumerski, our after-school baby-sitter, for a ride. I wouldn't miss dinner because we eat late anyhow, since Mom gets home from work late.

Everything was going fine until my sister (Kathie—she's only in third grade) saw that article in the newspaper. I wish she didn't like to read so much! But what's worse is that she has to tell everyone about what she reads.

I was all set to dive into my cherry pie after supper one night when Kathie said, "Hey, Mom, I just read a really good article in the *Times*. It's about how some football and baseball players take ballet lessons."

"Ballet lessons?" Mom asked, looking up.

"Ballet lessons!" I almost choked on a mouthful of cherries.

"Yes, ballet lessons," Kathie answered, "during the off-season to help them keep in shape. Some of them even do it during the playing season because it helps them be more graceful."

"Oh, next I suppose you'll say that I should take ballet lessons," I said, laughing real hard. "What a joke."

"Well," she said, looking at Mom and ignoring me, "our whole dancing school is going to do *The Nutcracker* for Christmas next year. The only trouble is there aren't enough boys, and I told Mrs. Goodwin that when baseball season ends, Mike would like to stay in shape and that he would come and . . ."

"You *what?*" This time I really did choke. "Me, dancing? No way!"

Mom glared at me. She turned to Kathie. "You know, dear, you mustn't promise something like that unless you ask Mike about it first."

Then she turned to me, and I could tell by the look in her eye that I was doomed. "However, Mike, it might be a good idea. You love music, and you complain that you don't get enough exercise during the winter."

"It's not winter now," I sputtered.

"No, but they really do need some tall boys practicing now to be ready to dance *The Nutcracker* at Christmas. Why don't you give it a try? If you don't like it after a month, you can drop it," Mom said.

I could tell by her tone of voice there was no use trying to talk her out of it.

So now, there I was, going to my first—ugh—

ballet lesson. If Jeff or Tim or any of the other guys had found out about it, I think I would have just died.

"Hey, Mom, can you call Jeff and tell him I'm sick or something? I was supposed to go over to his house tomorrow after practice, but now I've got that dumb dancing lesson."

"That won't be necessary, dear," Mom had said, giving me her you-know-we-don't-do-that-kind-of-thing look. "Jeff just called to say his uncle will be visiting him tomorrow, so it wouldn't work out anyway."

The next day Jeff was sure quiet at practice. He didn't even talk about his uncle coming, so I figured maybe he wasn't happy about it or something. After practice Coach Goodwin said to me, "Can I give you a lift to the dancing school?"

"Sh-h-h!" I hissed, looking around quick to make sure no one had heard him. "You mean *you're* going over there?"

"Sure," he said. "I teach the boys' class."

"You do?" I couldn't believe what I was hearing.

"Right," he answered. "I used to dance with a ballet company to stay on my toes, until I injured my knee. You know, you've got to be in excellent physical shape to be a good ballplayer and a good dancer. Dancers are just like any other kind of athlete."

When we reached Coach's car, I saw Jeff sitting in it, looking as miserable as I had felt earlier. Tim and some of the other guys were twirling around on their toes in the dust beside the car. "Jeff's going to dance like this," Tim hooted as he spun around. The rest of the guys were laughing.

Right then I wanted to run the other way, hop on my bike, and pedal home—fast. But Jeff sure looked all alone. And besides, if I had to go to dancing class, it would be a lot more fun to have one of my friends there, too. So I called out, "Hey, Jeff, did you know you have to be in great shape to be a good dancer? Some of the best ballplayers take ballet lessons to stay in shape for the season." Tim and the other guys just stood there in the dust. I guess they didn't know what to say about that.

Jeff grinned and looked a little happier. I never thought that anything Kathie said would make me or my friends feel better, but I'm glad I remembered her *Times* article.

Then I remembered something else. "Hey, Jeff, what about your uncle?"

Jeff rolled his eyes and smiled.

The Smallest Surfer

By Rick Boyes

It was a great day for surfing, and many young surfers were walking along the road to the beach. Each was carrying a surfboard. Some were blue, some were red, and many others had different colors.

"Teo! Hurry up, or we'll miss the contest!" yelled one boy. Nine-year-old Teo looked up at his big brother, Kala, and tried to run to him, lugging his heavy surfboard.

Teo was excited because Kala's club, the Surf Kings, was going to be in the surfing contest. The boys had been waiting several weeks for it. It was one of the big contests on the island of Maui in the state of Hawaii. Everyone in the Surf Kings wanted to win the first-place team trophy.

When Teo and his brother got to the beach, they found the others from the club. Teo stood proudly by his older brother. Kala was tall, with black hair and a deep tan. He was one of the leaders of the Surf Kings and one of the best surfers in town.

"Can I be in the contest?" asked Teo. He knew there was an event for his age group.

"No, Teo, we told you before. You are too small," said one boy.

"Maybe next year, Teo," said another. "You might not do very well and might hurt the club's chances for the first-place trophy."

Teo was disappointed. He had been watching Kala and learning from him how to ride a wave.

"All clubs, please sign up now!" called Mr. Lehua, a teacher at the school in town. He and two of his friends were the judges of the surfing contest. Soon five teams had written their names in the book. The contest was starting.

"Good luck, Kala!" shouted Teo. The older

surfers would be first. After a few minutes, Teo saw Kala standing on his surfboard, riding a wave to shore. He looked so strong and sure of himself. Teo cheered when he found out that Kala had won first place in his event.

As the day went on, each of the other age groups had a turn in the surfing contest. Near the end, the Surf Kings were in second place, right behind a team called the Daredevils. It was time for the nine-year-olds.

"I say that we let Teo try," said Kala. The others were not sure. They saw that the Daredevils were not sending in a nine-year-old. If Teo could place first or second, the Surf Kings would get the first-place trophy. If Teo came in third or fourth, the Surf Kings would end up in third place.

"Second place is okay if you have tried your best," Kala said to the other boys. "But we still have a chance for first. If we don't let Teo try, we're not very brave!" The boys looked at each other for a moment and then nodded their heads. Teo would try.

As Teo paddled out to the waves, he was remembering all Kala had taught him. He saw one boy try to stand up on the surfboard but slip off. "Don't watch the other surfers or the people on the shore," Kala had often told him. "You must watch only the wave and your board!"

Teo saw a good wave coming and got ready. He lay flat on his stomach. As he started to stand up, there were cheers on the shore. But Teo listened only to the sea and the surf. He was going faster and faster! The salty water sprayed his face. What would Kala do? Teo used his arms for balance the way his brother had shown him. He let his feet feel the wave under the board. Soon he was near shore and could see Kala's smiling face. The wave now took him gently to the beach. The ride was over.

The boys all stood around Teo. They were nervous. Some of the other nine-year-olds had done well also. Kala looked at Teo as Mr. Lehua called all the boys over.

"First place for the nine-year-olds goes to Rodney Kimura!" The Surf Kings groaned quietly. "Second place for the nine-year-olds goes to Teo Kealoha!"

The Surf Kings started to jump around and laugh. Their club had won the first-place trophy! Everybody was patting Teo on the back and hugging him. Kala put his arm around his brother and smiled at him. He seemed too proud of Teo even to speak. They walked over to the judges' stand to claim their trophy.

"You're a small boy, but a good surfer," said Mr. Lehua. Teo smiled shyly. Like his brother, he was too happy for words.

As the boys walked back along the road to town, Teo had very little trouble keeping up with them. Somehow his surfboard did not seem as heavy now. He thought about many things. He was happy for the Surf Kings, and even happier for making Kala proud of him. But he was happiest for himself because he had tried his best.

Dogsled Race

By Iris Klapka

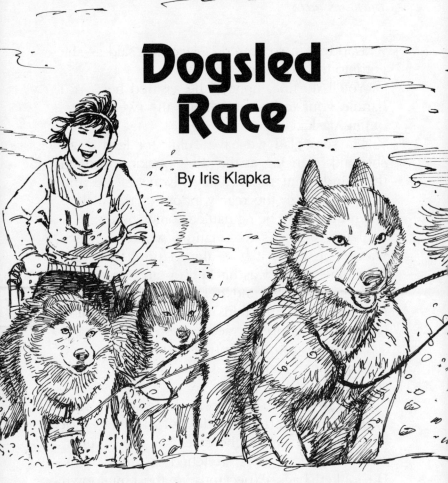

Maryanne checked her team and sled. The dogs, eager to get going, were restless. Their bushy tails curled high over their heads. While her father loaded the big sled, the dogs jumped into the straw-filled truck for the ride.

"Daddy, I'm so scared," Maryanne said as she got into the front seat.

"You'll do fine, honey," he assured her. "You handle your team better than any twelve-year-old in Alaska."

"I'm sure glad we have Tuluk for lead dog," she said, glancing at the dogs peeking through the window at them. They always stood and looked through the rear window of the pickup when they were being hauled somewhere.

At the Musher's Association, where the race was to be held, it was almost time to begin. Maryanne's team was hitched up and strung out in formation. She and her father checked and rechecked for faulty reins, harnesses, or anything that might foul up the race for her.

"Team number four!" came over the loudspeaker. "Maryanne Crane, with a team of seven dogs."

Maryanne could barely hold the eager animals. Her father would help till the shot signaling the start of the race was fired. Tuluk, Maryanne's lead dog, stretched the reins tight. He looked back expectantly as the countdown started. *Bang!* The shot sounded, and the team lurched forward.

Maryanne let the brake loose at the same instant. The sled and team went tearing along the packed snow trail toward the timber.

Maryanne hung onto the handles of the sled; her feet, clad in warm mukluks, were on the bottom bar.

"Faster, Tuluk," she urged the big, blue-eyed husky. "We have to win this race." In answer, the great dog pushed ahead, pulling the smaller dogs with him.

The wind was cold. Brush on the narrow trail hit Maryanne in the face, and the sled sped forward.

As they came around a turn, Maryanne saw a young moose standing directly in their path. Tuluk had seen many of these large animals and was not afraid. But the other dogs became confused and frightened. The moose jumped out of the way, but the damage had already been done. Although Tuluk tried valiantly to keep them in a straight line, some of the dogs went in one direction, while others went the opposite. The result was a whimpering, tangled pile of dogs and reins. In their attempt to right themselves, they succeeded only in becoming more entangled.

Maryanne quickly tied the ends of the reins to a sapling and started to straighten out the dogs and their ropes. She wasn't worried about her lost time now, but the safety of the other driver and the two teams of dogs.

The untangling was going so slowly that

Maryanne removed her gloves to get the reins separated. Her fingers soon became so cold that she could hardly use them. She could hear the dogs of the other team barking as they came closer. She worked desperately to get the last dog straight and in place. Finally, they were ready. "Tuluk, mush!" she commanded, and they moved quickly forward just as the next driver, an Eskimo boy, came up behind her, hard on her heels.

Maryanne held the lead for a little while, but at a broad turn the boy slid past her and her dogs, waving as he passed. He was helping his dogs by frequent pushes with his own feet on the ground.

The speed of his sled and team threw little snow showers in Maryanne's face. She had to depend upon her dogs to see where they were going. "Hurry, Tuluk," she begged. "Let's try to overtake them." She pushed as she had seen the Eskimo boy do.

The trail was about an hour's run for the average musher. Maryanne hoped she hadn't lost too much time untying knots in the pileup.

At last she saw the finish line and the crowd waiting to check the times of the drivers. Maryanne's father slowed the dogs down after they cleared the finish gate.

"What was my time?" she asked breathlessly.

"Did I make it under the hour?"

"Quite a bit under, honey," he told her proudly. "Fifty-two minutes, three seconds."

After what seemed hours, the mushers were all in and the final times tabulated. Maryanne had come in third.

"I'm so happy," Maryanne told her father excitedly. "Maybe I'll come in first next year. I'll just have to get the younger dogs used to the wild animals they may meet on the trails."

As her father helped her load the tired dogs into the truck, Maryanne gave Tuluk a special treat for his good work.

The Relay Race

By Isobel Morin

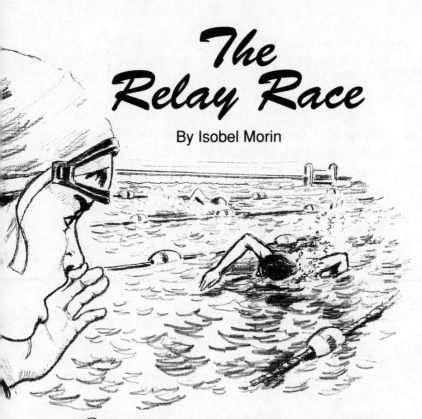

Chan shaded his eyes against the sun's glare and groped in his swim bag for sunglasses. Assistant Coach Lynne Marconi was about to announce Maple Grove's lineup for the Midstate Swim League Championships.

Chan could almost feel the cool metal of the three first-place trophies he would win. He had been practicing with the swim club since last fall, and his times had dropped dramatically. He held most of Maple Grove's records for his age group, and he had a lock on first place in most individual events.

Coach Marconi read from a typed sheet. "Age eleven and twelve boys' relay team—Tony De Luca, Jamie McLaine, Sam Levitt, Chan Lu."

Chan frowned. He didn't want to be on the relay team. If he swam the relay, he could swim only two individual events. The Maple Grove relay team wouldn't take first place anyway. The Riverside team was almost certain to beat them. He didn't want a second-place trophy when he could have a first. Chan scowled as he approached the coach.

She listened patiently before explaining her decision. "I need you on the relay, Chan. If you don't anchor it, we have no chance of placing in the top three. If you do, we have a good shot at second place."

Chan looked down at his toes, tracing circles in the grass. "But I can take three *first* places on my own."

"This is a team effort. By swimming the relay, you can help three others take home trophies. Will you do it?"

"All right," Chan agreed reluctantly.

The day of the championships was sunny and dry, with a high in the low eighties predicted—

ideal racing weather. Chan lay under the team's canvas shelter and waited for his races. As expected, he was seeded first in both the 100-yard individual medley and the 50-yard freestyle. There was only one problem. Sam was home with the flu. The Maple Grove relay was seeded second, but Rich Randall, the alternate for Sam, was a good two seconds slower. They would have to work hard just to place in the top three.

Chan easily won both of his individual races, but he was still disappointed about the relay. He wished the coach hadn't asked him to swim it.

It was past 2 P.M. when their relay was called. Tony, leading off, opened up a small lead over the Riverside swimmer. Jamie, swimming next, fell behind, but they were still a close second when Rich dived into the water. His lack of speed was immediately apparent. The Riverside swimmer widened his team's lead. Rich lost more ground on the turn. The Meadowbrook swimmer overtook him in the second lap, and the swimmer from Sunny Acres was gaining on him.

Chan jumped up and down on the starting block and waved his clenched fists. "Come on, Rich!" he yelled. "Kick harder! You're too slow!"

The Sunny Acres swimmer overtook Rich. Maple Grove was in fourth place, practically out of the running for a trophy.

Chan stamped his foot. I knew Rich would lose it for us, he thought.

As Rich neared the wall, Chan bent down, grabbed the block with both hands, and flew into the water. Stroking furiously, he went after the Sunny Acres swimmer. He caught up with him at the turn and pulled ahead in the second lap. As he neared the wall, he overtook the Meadowbrook swimmer. Chan swam hard to the finish, slapped the wall with one hand, and stood to catch his breath. He had moved the team into second place. Why weren't they cheering?

An official tapped him on the back as he pulled himself out of the pool. "You left the block too soon, son. You false-started. We had to disqualify your team. Sorry."

Grabbing his towel, Chan slunk away from Coach Marconi and the others and headed for the dressing rooms.

He felt a hand on his shoulder. It was Al Masters, Maple Grove's head coach. His face was serious.

"I saw the relay, Chan. I think you owe your teammates an apology."

"Why?" Chan demanded. He looked everywhere but at the coach. "Rich lost the race! He was too slow."

"Hold on, Chan. Remember, Rich was doing

his best. Your team had a sure third place if you hadn't false-started. But I'm more concerned about your behavior *before* you swam. You should have been cheering for Rich, but you were yelling at him."

Chan stared at the ground. Before he could respond to Coach Masters, Rich came over.

"Am I interrupting, Coach Masters?" he asked. "I need to talk to Chan."

Rich turned to Chan. "Sorry about being so slow. I guess I made you false-start. I cost you a trophy."

Chan felt his face redden. His ears were burning. He twisted the strap of his goggles around one finger. "I'm the one who should apologize," he mumbled. "I should have paid attention to what I was doing. And I shouldn't have yelled at you. I'm the one who's sorry."

Chan looked at Coach Masters after Rich left. "I'd better catch Coach Marconi and the others. I have something to say to them, too."

As he trotted away, Coach Masters called after him, "See you at practice tomorrow morning, Chan. Don't forget, eight sharp."

Chan caught up with Rich and tapped him on the shoulder. "Maybe we'll both do better next year," he said.

Sweet September

By Robert Anderson

Joanne could almost taste the cool September air. It was like all the things she liked best rolled up into one good taste.

She had been eleven years old for two whole days now. Today was the last day for fishing before school started. It gave her a kind of happy-sad feeling. The sad part was that the lazy days of doing mostly what she wanted would be over. The happy part was that she would be seeing her friends again every day at school and learning some new sixth-grade things. Joanne couldn't explain why, but learning new things gave her a good feeling inside.

Joanne crawled carefully through the willows on the bank of the creek and looked at the pool where her big trout lived. She had been trying to catch the fish for three years now. She had hooked it three times, and it had broken her line every time. Joanne told herself that if she hooked the fish today, she would play it very carefully and not be in too big a hurry to get it out. It would be her last good chance this season.

Joanne was as still as a stump while her eyes searched for the fish. She spotted it swimming slowly back and forth in the lower end of the pool. It was feeding on small insects that floated down the stream. The fish looked even bigger than Joanne had remembered, as it rose to the top of the water and sucked in a small grasshopper.

Joanne's heart was pounding hard now, and her hands shook a little as she carefully put a grasshopper on her hook. I'm going to get you today, Big Boy, she thought. She slowly reached out with her fishing rod, being careful to keep it over the bank where the fish couldn't see it. When she had the rod in just the right position, she flipped the grasshopper so that it splashed softly on the water at the head of the pool. The cast was a good one, and the hopper floated slowly toward the fish. When it reached the spot where the big trout had taken the other insect, Joanne realized she was holding her breath and waiting for the strike. But her grasshopper floated by the spot and on down the stream.

Joanne blew her breath out in a disappointed sigh and started to lift the hook out of the water for another cast. The big fish turned suddenly and smashed the grasshopper so fast that Joanne didn't even have time to think. She jerked the rod and hooked the trout.

When the fish felt the hook, it streaked upstream. Joanne let it run without trying to slow it down. She knew she had to let the springy strength of the rod tire the trout before she could even hope to land it. Reaching shallow water at the head of the pool, the trout turned and charged back downstream. Joanne quickly pulled in line so it stayed tight between her rod and the fish. The trout made the same run four more times. Failing to break loose, it began to leap from the pool, shaking its head and thrashing the water loudly.

Joanne's heart was in her throat, and she was shaking all over. She discovered that she was talking out loud to the fish. "Oh, please don't get off, Big Boy! And don't break my line again! Get tired, big trout, and let me land you. I'd be so proud to take you home."

After a time that seemed like hours to Joanne, the big fish began to tire. Its runs for freedom became shorter and weaker, and finally Joanne was able to lead it over to the shallow water at her feet.

It was a huge rainbow trout about twenty inches long. It lay there on its side, exhausted, the broad red stripe shining beautifully in the morning sun. Joanne looked at it and was thrilled. I've done it, she thought. I've finally caught old Big Boy! Now he's all mine!

She knelt at the edge of the water and gazed at the great fish that had been a part of her summers for so long. Past trips in search of the fish glided through her mind like a movie. She had spent hours lying in the shade of the willows, planning how to catch him. She had even dreamed about how it would be when she did it. And now the fish was hers! Old Big Boy had finally been outwitted. This was the way to end a summer vacation!

As the big trout lay there, Joanne felt a strange tightening in her chest. Slowly her hands began to move. Her right hand held the line, and her left slid down it to the hook in the trout's mouth. Joanne pushed gently down and backward, and the hook came free.

Old Big Boy didn't move for a few seconds, and then he slowly swam out into the deep water of the pool.

Joanne watched him disappear and stood up. She looked out over the meadow that was all green and gold in the September sun. A quail called softly. A crow sailed over on shiny black wings. A cock pheasant crowed and drummed his wings in the wild rose thicket. Joanne had never seen things look so beautiful!

Ski Tracks on Silver Bell

By Jean Heyn

Slipping from the chairlift at the top of Mt. Werner, Chip felt sure he would win. He had worked hard on his slalom turns all week, and now they were smooth and fast. After a quick run down the mountain to warm up, he'd be ready for any and all competition in the slalom race down Howelsen Hill. Winning the race

77

would make him Junior Champ of the Steamboat Springs Ski Club.

"I bet I could win with only one ski," he said to his younger brother, Roger.

"You'll win," said Roger, "the way you've been practicing."

They skied along the gentle slope from the lift to the headwall above Elk Meadows. Below them, the white flank of the mountain fell away steeply. On either side of the trail stood spruce laden with quilts of sparkling white. The bare branches of aspen, velvety with frost, looked like deer antlers in early spring. There was no sound. Nothing moved in all the vast expanse of snow and forest. The brothers were alone on the mountain.

"Come on! Let's go!" Chip said. He pushed hard on his poles and took off. Roger was close behind, and they dropped rapidly, making short, tight turns.

Before they reached Elk Meadows, Chip turned off onto Silver Bell, a little-known shortcut that ran steeply down through the trees. Halfway down he saw the tracks—odd tracks that ran off the edge of the trail into the woods, making deep marks in the soft snow. He checked his downward plunge with a quick turn, skidding to a stop.

"Look out!" Roger yelled. But he was too

close. The next moment they were down in a snowy tangle of skis, legs, and poles.

"What's the big idea?" Roger said as they sorted themselves out.

"Didn't you see those tracks? They headed straight into the woods. We'd better take a look."

"You don't have time, Chip. It's still a long way down."

"Just the same, we ought to see what's at the end of those tracks."

"Not me." Roger's voice quavered. "Let's get out of here. It's spooky way out here in the woods."

"You wait, then—I'll just be a minute," Chip said. He sidestepped back to the place where the tracks left the trail. Then he slid cautiously along them.

"What is it, Chip?" Roger called.

"A man. He's unconscious, and his leg looks broken!" Chip called back, staring at the figure sprawled to one side of a tree. He stooped down and touched the man's shoulder. He didn't move.

Chip climbed back onto the trail and then slid down to Roger. "When we reach the bottom, we'll report the accident. It'll be all right."

Roger shoved off, dropping into the next hollow. Chip crouched, then straightened up again. The light had changed. A snowflake fell on his nose. "Roger!" he shouted.

Roger stopped and looked back. "What's the matter now?"

"I have to stay here, that's all. The Ski Patrol will never find those tracks if it's snowing. But tell them to hurry. Tell them halfway down Silver Bell."

With Roger gone, Chip felt terribly alone. He began to wonder if he was missing the race. About now the crowd would be gathering on either side of Howelsen Hill. The timers and judges would be in their places on the course. The other skiers would be wound up like springs, waiting only for the timer's signal to zing through the gates.

The snow was coming down fast now, and Chip could barely see the tips of his skis. He stamped his feet to keep them warm and beat his arms about his chest. All at once he thought he heard something. Was it a muffled shout . . . or only his imagination? "Hello!" he shouted. "Anyone there?"

"Hello-o! Where are you?" came the answering cry.

"Here. Halfway down Silver Bell."

In seconds three members of the scarlet-jacketed Ski Patrol appeared. Big Matt was in the lead, dragging the first-aid toboggan. Big Matt was not only head of the Ski Patrol but also one-time Olympic skier and idol of every skier in Steamboat Springs.

"In there," Chip said, pointing.

"Good," said Big Matt, feeling for the downed skier's pulse. "Now, Chip, go on. The judges are trying to hold the race for you, but . . ."

Chip needed no coaxing. A jab of his poles sent him flying down the trail. The light was flat, making it hard to judge the terrain. He turned down Jack Rabbit Jumps, skiing hard and fast. The snow went by faster and faster. Suddenly his skis flew out from under him. He fell hard. A stab of pain shot up his left leg. He lay in the snow until the pain eased a little, then he rolled onto his back, straightened his skis, and brought them down parallel to the slope. Gingerly he pushed himself up with his poles and was off again.

At the bottom of Jack Rabbit Jumps, sun flooded the slopes. Through squinting eyes Chip saw the slalom course stretching below him. A figure was streaking down the course. Chip gritted his teeth. Was he too late?

He skied to the top of the slalom course and slid to a stop.

"Well, Carson," the judge said, "you're just in the nick of time. Are you ready to race?"

"Yes, sir." Chip stepped into the starting position.

81

The judge nodded to the timer, who looked at his stopwatch and began the countdown. "Five, four, three, two, one . . . go!"

Chip zoomed down the course. His skis bit the snow as he zigzagged through the gates— ten, fifteen, twenty. There were fifty-five in all. Though his knee hurt, he thought only of winning the race.

His friends cheered as he maneuvered around a pole, cutting close but not touching. Above the others, Chip heard Roger. "Faster, Chip! Faster!"

He had lost count of the gates now. He just saw them coming at him . . . to the left, touch pole, shift weight . . . to the right. Suddenly, his injured knee buckled beneath him. He fell, tumbling over and over, taking several gates with him. Chip was disqualified.

He was taken to the clinic to have his knee strapped, then home to rest. He tried to watch TV, but he couldn't stop thinking about the race. He'd lost. He'd had the best time—and then he fell—and he'd lost.

The doorbell rang. He heard his mother in the hall, then the stamping of heavy boots. A moment later Big Matt was standing in the doorway. Chip struggled to get up.

"Stay there," Big Matt said, walking over to Chip's chair and putting his hand on his shoulder. "How's the knee?"

"Okay," Chip said, grinning a little.

"Can you walk?"

"Sure!"

"Come on, then." Big Matt held out his hand.

Hanging onto him, Chip got to his feet. They started slowly toward the door. "Many skiers win races," Big Matt said, "but you're a cut above. I'd like to see you in my kind of work when you're older. We need people like you on the Ski Patrol."

"The Ski Patrol? Me?"

"Sure. You're a fine skier, and you have a compassionate heart. Now we're going to the hospital to see a friend of yours."

"I don't have any friends in the hospital," Chip objected.

"Sure you do. Remember the man on the mountain? His leg is badly broken, and he's suffering from exposure. But he wants to thank the boy with the big heart who rescued him on the mountainside."

The Girl Who Couldn't Stop Reading

By Nancy West

Sarah read everything she saw with words on it. At breakfast she read the backs of cereal boxes and learned about vitamins, minerals, and baseball players. Sarah loved baseball, second only to books, and planned to play for the Cubs when she grew up.

She also read the back page of her father's

newspaper at breakfast and was annoyed when he wiggled it, turning the page.

"Wait, Daddy," she said. "I'm not finished."

Twice a day she read the words on the toothpaste tube about how not to get cavities.

She read books as she walked to school, while everyone ran by her, whirling and shouting, throwing balls, teasing each other. Sometimes the noise made her lose her place on the page.

She read with one hand and one eye while she was taking off her coat and hat and mittens.

She read while she waited for the teacher to come into the room, while everyone else shouted or sailed paper airplanes. Sometimes the commotion made her lose her place on the page.

When class started, Sarah read everything Mrs. Anderson asked her to—and more.

And when Mrs. Anderson said they would be turning in six book reports this term and everyone else groaned, Sarah smiled. She could read six books standing on her head.

When Mrs. Anderson made a chart for the wall with a gold star for every book the children read, Sarah's row of stars went off the paper and all the way to the map of Asia.

Sarah's brother, Wiley, said he was getting tired of her reading all the time. "All I ever see of Sarah is the top of her head," he said. "I have the part in her hair memorized, but I never see her face. And she leaves books all over the place. She must have a book in every room of the house."

"I do," Sarah said.

"But why?" he asked her, shaking his head. "Why not just carry one book with you if you have to read all the time?"

"Because there are too many books I want to read," she said, "and I have to keep up with all of them all the time. So I keep *Mary Poppins* on the stairs—"

"I know," he said. "I tripped over it last night."

"And *Winnie the Pooh* in the bathroom, and *Francis Goes to School* in the dining room, and *Madeline* on the back porch, and *Donald Has a Difficulty* on the front porch, and *Frog and Toad Together* in the living room."

"And about a hundred books under your covers," Mother said. "Don't think I don't know you're in there reading with a flashlight when you're supposed to be asleep, young lady."

So it went all during the school year. Sarah had so many book reports that her file took up an entire drawer. Her gold stars marched around the room and up to the ceiling. She had to climb on a ladder to paste them up.

When anyone asked her what she wanted for

Christmas, she said, "GUESS."

And she got ten books.

When winter faded and the sun was higher and warmer, the snow melted and the leaves came popping out on the trees. It was baseball season.

Sarah went home and put down her books. She reached under the bed and pulled out her cap, her glove, and her bat. She loved baseball. She could hit okay, and her arm was good, but she wasn't as good as she wanted to be at the game she loved so much.

Wiley stood and glared at her, hands on his hips, when she made errors during neighborhood games. And some of the other kids yelled at her.

So Sarah started reading about baseball. She read Ted Williams's book, *The Science of Hitting*. She read a biography of Babe Ruth. She read *The Roger Clemens Story* and *How to Play Better Baseball,* and she cried over a story about Lou Gehrig.

Now when she played second base, she knew where to throw the ball when she caught it on the bounce with one out and a runner at third. Now she knew how to run up on a grounder. Now she held her head still when she swung at the ball, never taking her eyes off it—and her batting average went up 100 points.

"I have to admit it," Wiley said, "I guess all that reading helped you improve a lot."

And Sarah noticed that he started carrying paperback books in *his* back pocket, too. She just smiled at him and hitched up her jeans, waiting for just the right ball before swinging the bat. Just like Babe Ruth.

Sea Legs

By Carolyn Bowman

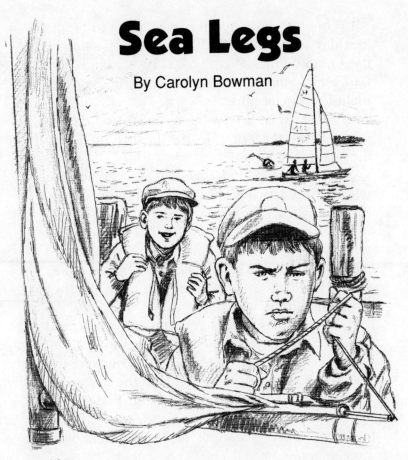

Casey leaped from the dock to his boat,
Jaws. He fitted the mast and sail on properly
while his brother Benji sat watching. Benji's eyes
were as big as half dollars. Benji was excited.
Casey was boiling mad.

Up until an hour ago this was going to be the best day of his life. The last race of the summer, the Commodore's Race, would be starting soon. Casey had sailed it in his dreams almost every night for two months.

In his dreams, he was alone in his red dinghy just out past the buoy. In his dreams, he'd won the race every time.

Now all that had changed. It was his mother who had changed it. "Take your brother along. It's time to teach him about racing."

Benji was all right as a sailor, but he had been sailing for only one summer and he had never raced. With an inexperienced first mate, Casey stood little chance of winning. His brother would get in the way.

Benji jumped to his feet on the dock and yelled, "Can I board now? Can I get on?"

"Not yet!" Casey snapped. He checked the small ties that fitted the sail to the boom. A quarter of an inch separated them. Perfect. He slipped on his life jacket.

"Now?" Benji pleaded, his eyes bright with excitement.

"Now," Casey mumbled as Benji stepped lightly aboard and settled against the stern, buckling on his life jacket too.

"Move," Casey said. "I have to work the tiller." Benji smiled and moved easily to the bow.

The wind was blowing out of the channel, and the sail billowed as Casey turned the boat away from the dock. They led the fleet of nine dinghies out to the committee boat.

"This is fun!" Benji yelled, making Casey angrier than ever. That was no way for a real sailor to act.

The Commodore waved as they pulled up to his starboard side. "I see your brother is getting his sea legs today."

Casey just frowned as he and Benji bobbed up and down on the choppy water, waiting for the starter's signal.

"It's going to be rough," Casey said, studying the whitecaps. "Just stay low and out of the way."

"Can I work the mainsheet?" Benji begged. He started to reach for the line.

"No way!" Casey said. "It's my race!"

The three-minute starting sequence began, and Casey sculled into position, moving his tiller left and right. *Bang!* The gun was fired, and they were off.

Casey turned *Jaws* to leeward, trying to catch the wind. The boat heeled and nearly went over. Little boats like Casey's capsized a lot. It didn't upset him or Benji, but if they did go over, it would mean precious moments lost while they worked to right *Jaws* in the water.

Two boats passed Casey's. Soon it would be too late to catch up. His boat heeled again, and Casey hiked out, sitting on the port side and leaning so far out that his back brushed the water. He used all his weight to bring the mast upright again.

One of the boats in front of him went over, its mast going straight down. Casey passed the capsized boat and headed for the only other dinghy in front of him. As they rounded the first mark, they came close to taking the lead.

"Let me help!" Benji yelled. "I'll take the mainsheet so you can hike out better!"

The other dinghy pulled farther ahead. Behind them, the rest of the boats sailed as a tight fleet. They were gaining, but slowly. Casey bit his lip. "No! I can do it myself!"

Just then, his sail caught an unexpected puff of wind and the boat heeled until the tip of his mast brushed the water.

"Hike with me, Benji!" Casey yelled. Benji leaped to the starboard side. He nestled in close to Casey and leaned back. Slowly, the mast pulled up and away from the rough sea.

The leading boat caught the same puff, but the skipper was alone and struggled to right his mast. Casey pulled up alongside him, hauled in the mainsheet, and shoved the tiller to try to move ahead.

"I can help!" Benji said. Casey looked at his little brother for a moment. He didn't want to let go of the mainsheet. But in the next boat sailed the one person who could take away Casey's dream of winning the race.

"Take it, Benji!" Casey said, and he shoved the line into Benji's hands. "Do exactly what I say!" Benji nodded as a spray of salt water slapped his face. As they rounded the second mark, they jumped to the port side and headed straight toward the finish line.

The two boats sailed together for most of the distance. Casey watched the sky, looking for clues, and saw his moment.

"Close haul her!" he yelled to Benji. It was their one chance to take the lead. The other skipper made the same move, but alone he was no match for Casey and Benji. "Hike out!" Casey yelled, and Benji leaped into position.

The other boat's mast caught the water and went over, throwing its skipper into the churning sea. As the boy climbed onto his boat and began to right it, Casey and Benji pulled into the lead for good. They crossed the finish line, and the gun sounded.

"We did it!" Casey yelled, and he punched Benji's arm. "We won the race!"

While sailing back to the club, Casey started to thank Benji but just couldn't find the right words. He had been so sure he could win the trophy all by himself. It was hard to admit that if Benji hadn't been along, he wouldn't have had a chance.

On the dock of the yacht club, the Commodore stood at the microphone. "This year's trophy," he announced, "goes to Skipper Casey Jones Webster."

When Casey walked up to accept his award, he took Benji's hand and pulled him along. "And his first mate, Benji," Casey added.